WAITING FOR SPACESHIPS

SCENES FROM A DESERT COMMUNITY IN LOVE WITH THE SPACE SHUTTLE

TED HUETTER

Fonthill Media Inc.
www.fonthillmedia.com
office@fonthillmedia.com

First published 2024

Copyright © Ted Huetter 2024

ISBN 978-1-62545-135-4

All rights reserved. No part of this publication may be reproduced, stored
in a retrieval system or transmitted in any form or by any means, electronic,
mechanical, photocopying, recording or otherwise, without prior permission in
writing from Fonthill Media Inc.

Typeset in Trade Gothic
Printed and bound in England

FOREWORD

I first visited Edwards Air Force Base in June 1976, as an Air Force Academy cadet making a pilgrimage to the holy city of flight testing, the Air Force Flight Test Center and NASA's Dryden Flight Research Center. Here the jet age had taken shape, with the Air Force's test pilots wringing out everything from the P-59 Airacomet (America's first jet fighter), to the supersonic X-1, a flock of pioneering X-planes, the Century Series jet fighters of the 1950s, and the sleek hypersonic X-15.

For a novice flier like me, with only a few dozen hours of glider time in my logbook, Edwards was a storied wonder, where the most advanced flying machines in history had taken flight. Here I glimpsed some of the planes I might one day take aloft. Being put through their paces were the F-16 Fighting Falcon, the F-15 Eagle, the B-1A bomber, the A-10 Thunderbolt II, and a pair of experimental jet transports, the YC-14 and -15. I imagined one day climbing into the cockpits of these cutting-edge jets, steps toward my ultimate dream of spaceflight.

That dream was taking shape just 37 miles south of the Edwards flight line, at Palmdale's Plant 42. Inside the cavernous factory, my group toured the hangar bay where the prototype space shuttle, *Enterprise*, was taking shape. *Enterprise* was the first of NASA's fleet of shuttle orbiters, and this first ship would prove the concept of gliding a 100-ton spaceship, power-off, to a precision landing at Edwards. In a series of five approach and landing tests in 1977, *Enterprise* did her job, clearing the way for the reentry of the first space-qualified orbiter, *Columbia*.

That first shuttle flight, STS-1, saw *Columbia* landing at Edwards' Rogers Dry Lake on April 14, 1981. The base's expansive dry lakebed provided a safety margin should the shuttle encounter trouble during its gliding approach. Fortunately, the orbiters were as reliable gliders as they were spaceships, and astronauts were soon piloting the shuttle to pinpoint concrete runway landings at Edwards.

I first met the shuttle at Edwards on May 16, 1992, when, as an astronaut family escort, I helped welcome home the STS-49 *Endeavour* crew, returning from OV-105's first flight. Standing alongside Runway 22 with the crew's families, we took in the breathtaking sight of *Endeavour* dropping steeply out of the sky and soaring nose up to a gentle touchdown.

Dan Brandenstein and Kevin Chilton set *Endeavour* down almost lovingly, with only a puff of vaporized rubber showing where the main gear first touched the concrete runway. After an exuberant reunion and post-flight physicals, the crew and their families repaired over dirt roads to the Silver Saddle guest ranch for a day of welcome rest. How I craved my own trip!

Soon enough, it was my turn, also on *Endeavour*, in April 1994. My STS-59 crew soared 4.7 million miles on 183 orbits. Unfavorable Florida weather forced us to choose Edwards for a landing site, and Sid Gutierrez and Chilton brought our ship in for an exhilarating approach over the Sierra Nevada and on into Edwards. From my right rear seat on the flight deck, I craned for a glimpse of the tan lakebed and gray concrete runway during the final seconds of our plunge toward Earth. The orbiter rumbled and shook as the desert air rushed over its slab sides and knobby tail, yet Sid confidently put us down on the approach end of 22 with a bare whisper of contact. My grin was a mile wide—I'd returned from space and a successful mission. Another, please!

Twice more, Florida's rain and clouds directed my shuttle crews to Edwards, on STS-68 and STS-98. Back from the Space Station in 2001 on that final mission, *Atlantis* sliced through low clouds and whipped to a perfect touchdown with Ken Cockrell and Mark Polansky doing the flying. I was elated—we'd pulled off three spacewalks to deliver the Destiny lab to the Station, and the Edwards staff welcomed us home with open arms.

Next morning, with spaceship *Atlantis* parked nearby, I crossed the Dryden flight line to visit the plane I'd piloted for five years—the Boeing B-52, this one a B-model, "*Balls 8*," operated by NASA as an X-plane mothership. The two aircraft—*Atlantis* and the B-52—were separated in time by nearly a half-century, yet they both called Edwards home. Here I first glimpsed a space shuttle being born, first watched one wing gracefully back to Earth, and first experienced the elation of returning to my home planet.

Ted Huetter's crisp, whimsical photos put you on the lakebed to welcome home a returning shuttle. His images transport us with thousands of Americans to a magical place in the California high desert. Here, flight test pioneers wrote the book on high-speed flight. Here, the space shuttle returned from fifty-four orbital missions. And here, I believe, we'll again see another generation of spaceships take flight and complete their journeys, welcomed home by crowds of dreamers and future explorers. At Edwards, extraordinary feats remembered propel us toward our destiny—above.

Tom Jones, planetary scientist, pilot, author, and veteran NASA astronaut

CONTENTS

	Foreword	3
	Acknowledgments	6
	Introduction	7
1	At Home on the Lakebed	17
2	Day of the Shuttle	83

ACKNOWLEDGMENTS

Thank you to the people who believed in this photo project and encouraged me to see it through, especially Patti Campbell, Cynthia Kirk, Mark Buntzman, Anca Colbert, Sarah Cruddas, Ken Phillips, Gale Elston, Bill Baxley, Jim Slavin, Kevin Elston, Russell Munson, Deborah Drouin, Tom Jones, Ingo Bauernfeind, Bruce McCaw and Craig Howard. Thanks to Carla Thomas and Kevin Rohrer at NASA Armstrong Flight Research Center for archival photo support, and at Fonthill Media I thank Kena Smith for editorial guidance and Jay Slater for bringing the book onboard. I also offer warm gratitude to Maki Gemma for her enduring patience during the home stretch of this project

INTRODUCTION

During the 1980s hundreds of thousands of people drove to a parched parcel in California's Mojave Desert to see spaceships glide to Earth. Many camped overnight, creating temporary communities with populations rivaling any non-coastal town in the state. It was during the first decade of NASA's thirty-year space shuttle program.

Beginning in April 1981, the shuttle "orbiters" were launched from NASA Kennedy Space Center in Florida, and for the next ten years the primary landing location was at Edwards Air Force Base in California—470 square miles of wild desert protecting the nation's top complex for military test flight operations. Edwards had secrets. Next stop, Area 51. Yet for years Edwards opened its gates to the public on the day before an orbiter was set to land. Shuttle fans were directed to an isolated patch of hard, flat clay that offered clear views of the runways. There were no security checks, and the military presence at the "Shuttle Landing Viewing Site" was more about assistance than resistance. Visitors were welcome to stay until the shuttle was on the ground. Those were precious times.

I was there for eight shuttle landings from 1982 through 1989. My photographs are reminders of the site's quiet beauty, quirky charm, and unabashed displays of Americana. The images depict a composite twenty-four hours at the settlement, from the first campers' arrival to the shuttle's touchdown.

Located about thirty to forty miles south of Edwards Air Force Base, the small Antelope Valley towns of Palmdale and Lancaster were home to many of the aerospace contractors and NASA employees who supported the orbiter program. The shuttles were built at the Rockwell International plant in Palmdale. Lancaster's Antelope Valley Inn motel expressed civic pride on the day space shuttle *Columbia* made its first landing. [*NASA photo*]

GRAVITATING TO THE SHUTTLE

When the Soviet Union's tiny satellite, Sputnik, beep-beep-beeped around the Earth in 1957, spaceflight became real, the United States felt threatened, and the race began. The 1960s Space Race to put "men on the moon" was a vast spectacle on an international stage. America won in 1969, then suspended the Apollo lunar flights two and half years later, and the U.S.S.R. focused on long-duration Earth-orbiting flights in their Salyut space stations. Despite technical setbacks and tragic fatalities, the Salyut program progressed. The Soviets found their niche.

Meanwhile NASA cleverly developed America's first space station using a leftover moon rocket. Skylab launched in May 1973, and during the next nine months, the cavernous orbiting laboratory was home to three-man crews during three different missions. That was it for Skylab and NASA's crewed spaceflights for a couple more years.

Throughout all of this, the rival spacefaring nations set their differences aside and planned a joint mission geared around a rendezvous of orbiting U.S. and U.S.S.R. spacecraft. In 1975 three astronauts in an Apollo spacecraft docked with two cosmonauts in a Soyuz spaceship. International television broadcasts beamed live video as the crews exchanged pleasantries and fielded questions from the home planet. The Apollo-Soyuz Test Project was the last crewed spaceflight for the Americans until the first shuttle mission almost six years later, while the Soviets kept orbiting in bigger and better space stations.

The delayed NASA shuttle program finally launched in April 1981. Two astronauts flew the shuttle *Columbia* on a two-day orbital test hop. Liftoff was at NASA Kennedy Space Center and the landing was at Edwards Air Force Base. Edwards offered the world's longest runways and was the safest place to land virtually anything. The base was also the home of NASA Hugh L. Dryden Flight Research Center (renamed NASA Neil A. Armstrong Research Center in 2014), which was fully equipped to handle space shuttle operations during the orbiter's arrival and post-landing processing. Dryden crews could also shuttle the shuttle to Kennedy on the back of a modified Boeing 747 that NASA prosaically named the Shuttle Carrier Aircraft. (Is it surprising that the apparatus NASA used to lift the shuttle on and off the SCA was called the Mate-Demate Device?)

Columbia's success put America back in the crewed spacecraft business. A fleet of four additional shuttles were under development with a goal of making spaceflight as routine as air travel. The glorious Moon landings seemed ages ago, so the American public optimistically embraced the shuttle program. Launches and landings were TV news events. Ronald Reagan was the new President. The Cold War was heating up. The U.S. space program was again riding high.

GRAVITATING TO THE DRY LAKE

The Army Air Corps first staked out the future Edwards Air Force Base in the early 1930s for bombing and gunnery practice. Although the land was only 100 miles north of Los Angeles, it was still in the middle of nowhere. Facilities were established there during World War II to train aircrews for overseas duty. During the war it also became the secret test site for America's first jet fighter, the Bell Airacomet. Before long it was the Air Force's top spot for testing new airplanes. In 1946 NASA's predecessor, the National Advisory Committee for Aeronautics (NACA), established a permanent presence there to work with the Air Force on the first supersonic airplane, the X-1. The partnerships and supporting infrastructures grew with the evolution of more exotic and sophisticated flying machines. The NACA became NASA in 1958. Edwards remained the agency's home base for aeronautical flight research.

Edwards test pilots were said to have "the right stuff." NACA and NASA test pilots mounted experimental planes to methodically probe new realms of flight. Military test pilots wrung out every potential aircraft in the nation's arsenal. Most of the Apollo and space shuttle astronaut pilots got their chops at Edwards. Today it is home to NASA Armstrong Flight Research Center, the Air Force Flight Test Center, the Air Force Test Pilot School, and includes outposts for virtually all major players in the American aerospace field. And they are all there because of its clear skies above a vast prehistoric landscape centered on an expanse of flat desolation called Rogers Dry Lake.

The radical flights at Edwards sometimes go haywire, demanding quick emergency landings; some of the weird aircraft flown there simply need more wriggle room for takeoffs and descents; and exotic gliders like the shuttle have one shot at landing, so multiple runway options are a big plus. Rogers Dry Lake is a forty-square-mile target with landing opportunities in any direction. Edwards' main concrete runway stretches almost three miles along one shore, while another sixteen runways are drawn directly on the hard playa of Rogers and adjacent Rosemond Dry Lake. The longest landing option extends seven and a half miles (that's almost four times the length of runway at a major international commercial airport). From the air these epic desert earthworks possess an abstract quality and scale that reminds me of the ancient lines etched into the desert near Nazca, Peru. And both of these totemic places are visible from orbit. Hopefully the Edwards lines will be preserved for future generations to enjoy from space long after they've served any practical purpose. Back in the 1980s though, when shuttle flights were always a bit experimental, the big sketches at Edwards brought some comfort to the orbiter crews down the home stretch.

Miles of runway and navigational markings on the Mojave Desert's Rogers Dry Lake, dating to 1940 AD. [*NASA photo*]

Miles of runway-like markings on the Nazca Desert near Nazca, Peru, dating to 200 BC–700 AD. [*Author photo*]

THE SHUTTLE LANDING VIEWING SITE

There were many reasons people came to Edwards to watch a shuttle land on American soil, but first and foremost is simply that they could. Before shuttle orbiters, all crewed U.S. spacecraft "splashed down" in seas far from the U.S. mainland and were recovered by the U.S. Navy. There was no way the average person could be there. Watching live TV coverage was as close as it got. Finally, after twenty years of spaceflight it was possible for regular, non-NASA, non-military, non-VIP folks to personally witness a spaceship returning to Earth. The only snag was that they had to watch from a harsh patch of desert about three miles from the runway.

Most of the people I talked to at the Edwards Space Shuttle Viewing Site said they were there because they wanted to be a part of history or see history in the making. American history for sure. An experience to share with friends and family.

Some spectators came because they had helped build the shuttles at Rockwell International's manufacturing plant at Palmdale Airport about 40 miles south of Edwards. Some of the orbiter technicians had previously worked on the Apollo spacecraft in Southern California, but only saw those fly on television like everyone else. The shuttle landings at Edwards gave them the opportunity to personally taste the fruits of their labor.

Many viewers came from greater Los Angeles. The drive to Edwards was only a couple hours or so, and the desert destination had an exotic appeal. Adventurous retirees from around the country made Florida to California treks in their recreational vehicles, book-ending the trips with a shuttle launch and landing.

Space devotees at the site believed that the shuttles were the beginning of a thrilling new era in spaceflight that would include you and me on commercial passenger trips. The roomy shuttle seemed to be the logical evolution of space transportation after the tiny, parachute-landing Apollo capsules. This was the New Space Age.

The Air Force gates opened to the public on the day before a scheduled shuttle landing. The viewing site was on an edge of Rogers Dry Lake a few flat miles from the Edwards main runways and support complex. The area was defined with seemingly endless rows of widely spaced tar-painted parallel lines bordered by a low, flimsy fence. Everyone parked along the lines. A wide promenade stretched between the fence and the front row of vehicles.

The military supplied an abundance of potable water tanks, portable sanitary facilities, generators, streetlights, a first aid station, and a command post. Air Force personnel directed traffic and patrolled the avenues, but generally kept a low profile and friendly presence.

An estimated 500,000 people were at the shuttle landing viewing site on the morning of the July 4, 1982. President Ronald Reagan was among the VIPs in attendance at the NASA Dryden (now Armstrong) Flight Research Center. [NASA photo]

Food and souvenir vendors were the first arrivals at the site, and they quickly established a centrally located bazaar. Campers were directed to claim spaces in an orderly, linear fashion beginning with the rows closest to the lakebed fence. Park and get settled was the routine. Overnighters quickly set up household, then kicked back and watched the neighborhood grow. The vehicles stayed put, so the spaces behind each row of campers became wide walkways. It was a peaceful community that strolled a lot.

Folks visited, meandered, and shopped. The kids played. Despite the weird mosaic of recreational vehicles, military jeeps and vendor booths, it was Our Town, U.S.A. Life was uncomplicated and crime-free. Strangers mingled freely. Eccentricities flowered. The American flag was everywhere.

Day temperatures could be brutally hot. Relatively few campers had the luxury of air conditioning, so folks tended to stay outside cloaked in whatever shade they could devise. Clearly lots of adults preferred to stay hydrated by drinking generous quantities of beer and cocktails, yet I never saw any rowdiness. The pace was slow in an old-timey way. Maybe the military presence had something to do with it, but I like to think that the power of the desert environment had a calming effect. It seemed only the kids moved very fast.

The community perked up as shadows lengthened and temperatures dipped. There was a quiet bustle to the place. Browsing and shopping were brisk. The avenues became playgrounds. Eventually the scattered thousands reversed course and came home for dinner. Barbeques smoked and propane stoves hissed.

The dimly lit bazaar served as a lively downtown destination for a few hours after dark. Air Force streetlights glared all night, but beyond the site the surrounding expanse quickly faded to black. The small town of Edwards glowed softly on one horizon, and the crystalline desert sky revealed a profound depth of stars. Astronomy nerds with telescopes welcomed everyone to their star parties. At night, the orbiting shuttle astronauts didn't seem so far away.

The shuttle landings at Edwards were usually planned for morning, when the air was calm and cool. Some campers got up early to partner with the promise of dawn. Word spread quickly with the latest news about the shuttle's position and ETA. When the orbiter was finally committed to its final orbit—arrival ninety minutes and counting—people settled into place. Those with large recreational vehicles, vans, and buses climbed to their rooftop sky boxes; the rest would cozy up to the perimeter fence. Hundreds of portable radios were tuned to the same live coverage of NASA mission control. Their tiny speakers became a sprawling public address system.

When the shuttle was ten minutes from Edwards, its twin sonic booms hit coastal cities 100 miles away. Car alarms sounded, dogs barked, and earthquake fears were triggered in more than a few Californians.

Columbia made the first orbiter landing at Edwards Air Force Base on April 14, 1981. This photo captures the shuttle on its final descent to Rogers Dry Lake. [NASA photo]

At five-and-a-half minutes to touchdown, the shuttle was 80,000 feet high and sixty miles from the runway. The lakebed community anxiously searched the skies. Even when the orbiter was only a few minutes away, it was still out of sight. Then some eagle-eyed fans spotted its tiny, arrowhead shape. Arms shot up, pointing. Scattered shouts punctured the droning of the radios: "There it is! There it is! Where? There! I don't see it! There! There!" In a beat the orbiter's shock waves slammed everyone with a quick bam-BAM! Now there was cheering, and the spacecraft miraculously appeared as a speedy black point about three miles up in a ridiculously big sky.

The clamor gave way to a soothing calm. The echo of countless radios became a faint white noise. Eighty seconds until landing. The sky seemed bigger than ever and connected directly to the heavens. The shuttle's glide was graceful yet aggressively steep. It had a brutal beauty.

Most of us have endured a "minute of silence" surrounded by a congregation of strangers with eyes reluctantly shut and heads awkwardly bowed. The shuttle community shared sixty seconds in reverential peace with heads up and eyes focused on something rare and awesome. It was a powerful, deeply personal silence. Most didn't cheer when the spaceship touched the Earth. They were too choked up.

Public attendance for each of the early shuttle landings drew hundreds of thousands. Numbers declined over the next five years as the flights became commonplace, but the community endured. Then Space Shuttle *Challenger* exploded shortly after liftoff. The remaining shuttle fleet was grounded for two years. The first flight of the resurrected orbiter program brought the multitudes back to Edwards, then the novelty wore off again, and the viewing community's population settled into to a cozy five or ten thousand per landing.

In 1992, Kennedy Space Center replaced Edwards as the shuttles' primary landing port. And the lakebed viewing site became another sort of ghost town in the American West.

Expansive Rogers Dry Lake and intersecting runways. After landing, the shuttle was towed several miles to the NASA Dryden Flight Research Center located at the edge of the lakebed. [NASA photo]

1

AT HOME ON THE LAKEBED

The Last Highway

Base Road

Final Turn

The Arrival

Spotless

An Abundance of Facilities

Visitors This Side/Air Force That Side

Air Force Ops

Choice Location

Basic Provisions

Astroturfers

22

Common Awning

Choice Sunshine

Top Dog

Couples

Cancer Cures Smoking

Len Jr

Superior

Desert Serenade

Car Following

27

A Pause in the Conversation

Radio and Parasol

We Love

Welcome Home Atlantis

Shuttle on Wheels

Hats

Precious Shade

Mobile Travelers

Vintage Voyagers

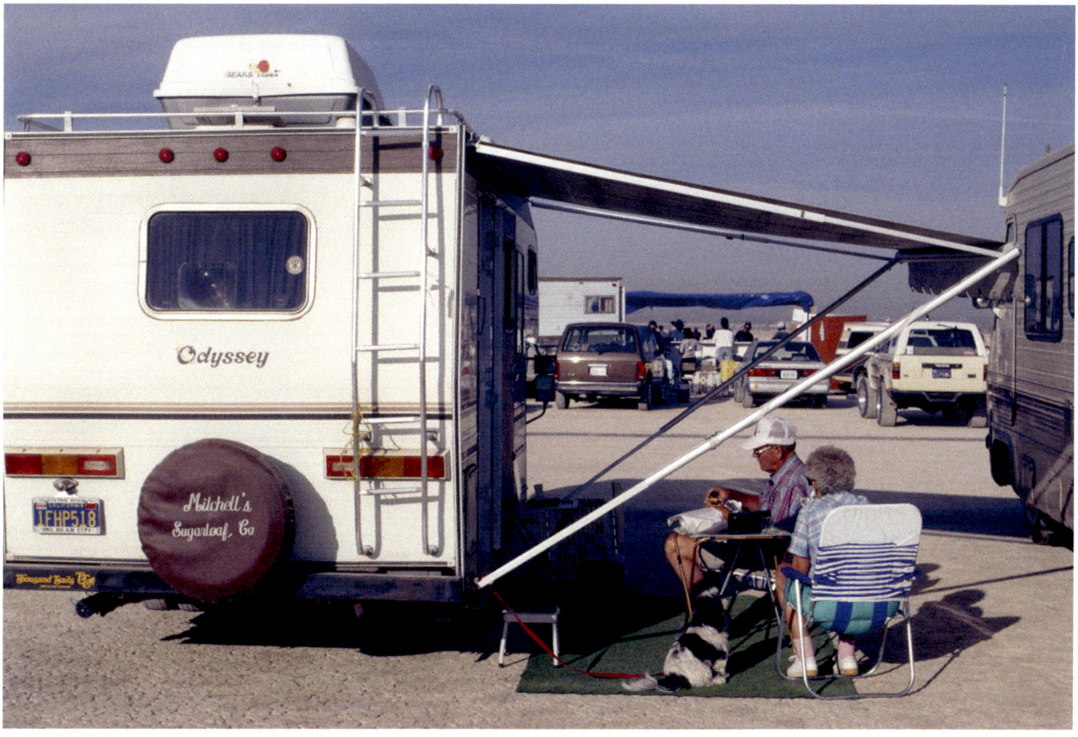

Snack Time for the Mitchells

Scotsman Shade

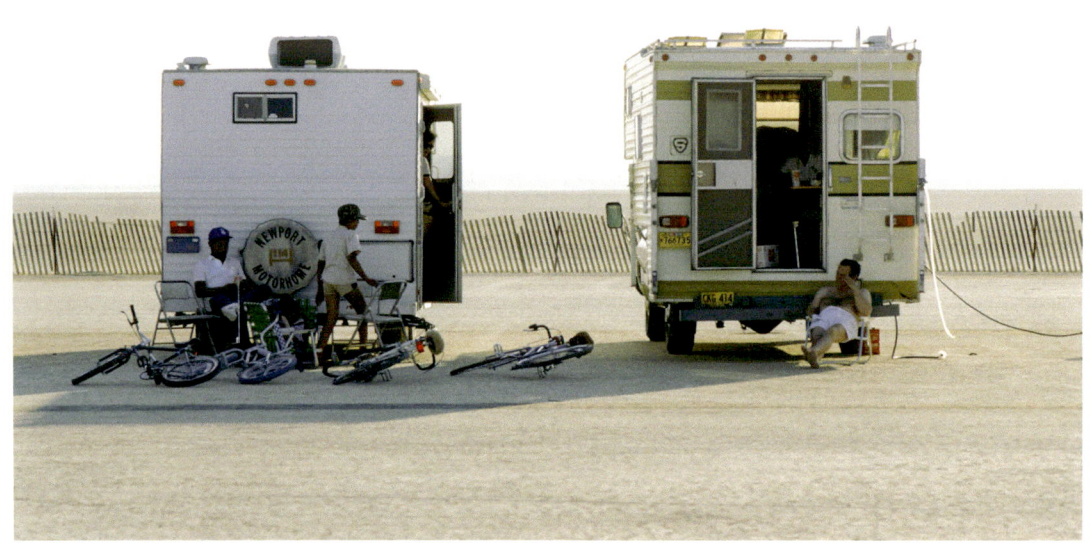

Bike Rest

Pearl Harbor Survivor

We Were There!

Pushing Souvenirs

Calligrapher

Inside Cokes

Pins and Pin Wheels

Shorts

Boots

Let Freedom Ring

Guts

A Glorious Breeze

History for Sale

41

Olympics 84

Tomorrow's News Today

Shuttle Love

Marilyn

Shirt Sail

Six Bucks Four Bucks

Cost Cutters

Remember Vietnam

STS-4

Space Transportation

Shuttle Hugger

We're Back

Sweats

Dayglow

Private Enterprise

Eight Bucks

America Returns

Shuttle Shadows

Michael

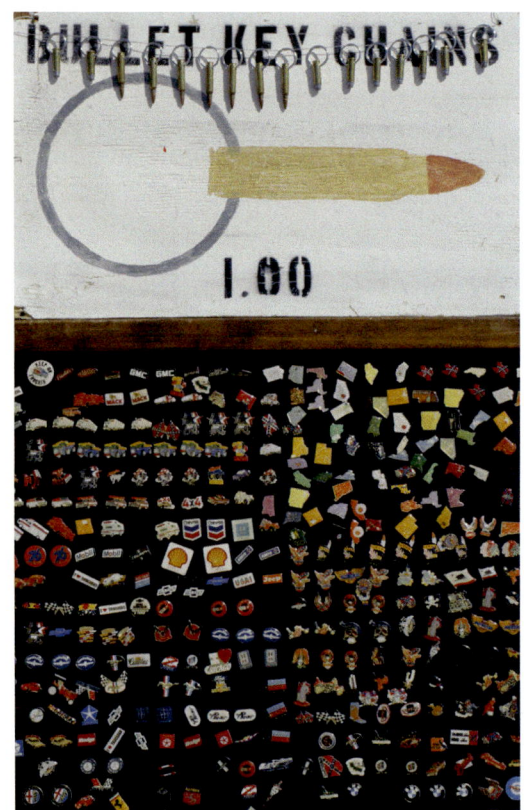

One Dollar

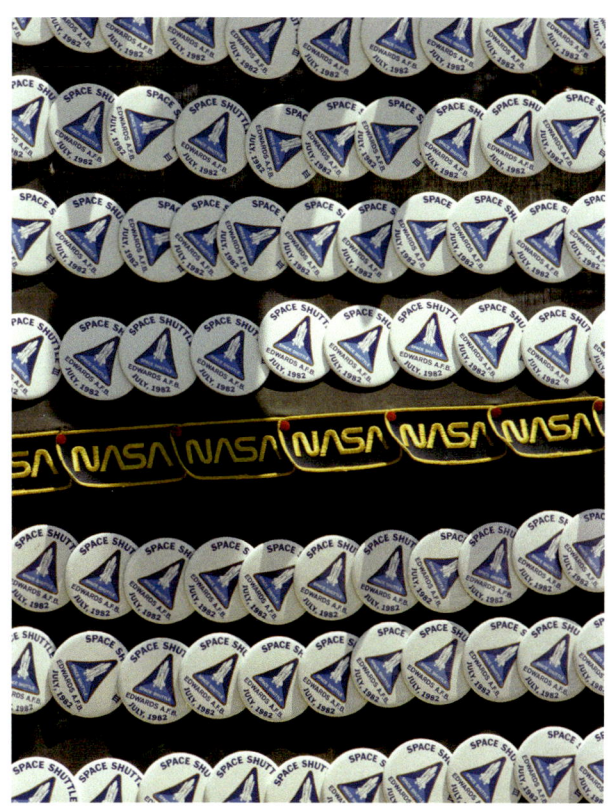

July 1982

At Edwards

Gateway

Army Chow

MWR

Killer Tees

White Walls

Kite Girl

Riding Fences

No Sweat

Dune Buggy Patriots

To the Moon

Retired

Good Sam

Chuck Wagon

Ready for Tomorrow

Talk Show

Documentary

Family Portrait

Independence

Steak

Mr. Rollout

Boys on the Bed

Walkman and Troops

Private Property

From Roseville

Wired

Bites

Neighbors

Rogers Roller

Portable Television

The Front Row

71

Running Home

Playtime with MPs

Silly Strings

Trios

Playa Vista

Low Attendance

Anybody Home?

Speed Boats and Dry Lake

75

Quiet Escape

AFCC Coffee

Territorial Views

First Aid

77

Generator on the Perimeter

Pooch

Snap

Something's Up

It's the Best

2
DAY OF THE SHUTTLE

Securing the Lakebed

To the West

To the East

Welcome Home Discovery

A Morning Concert

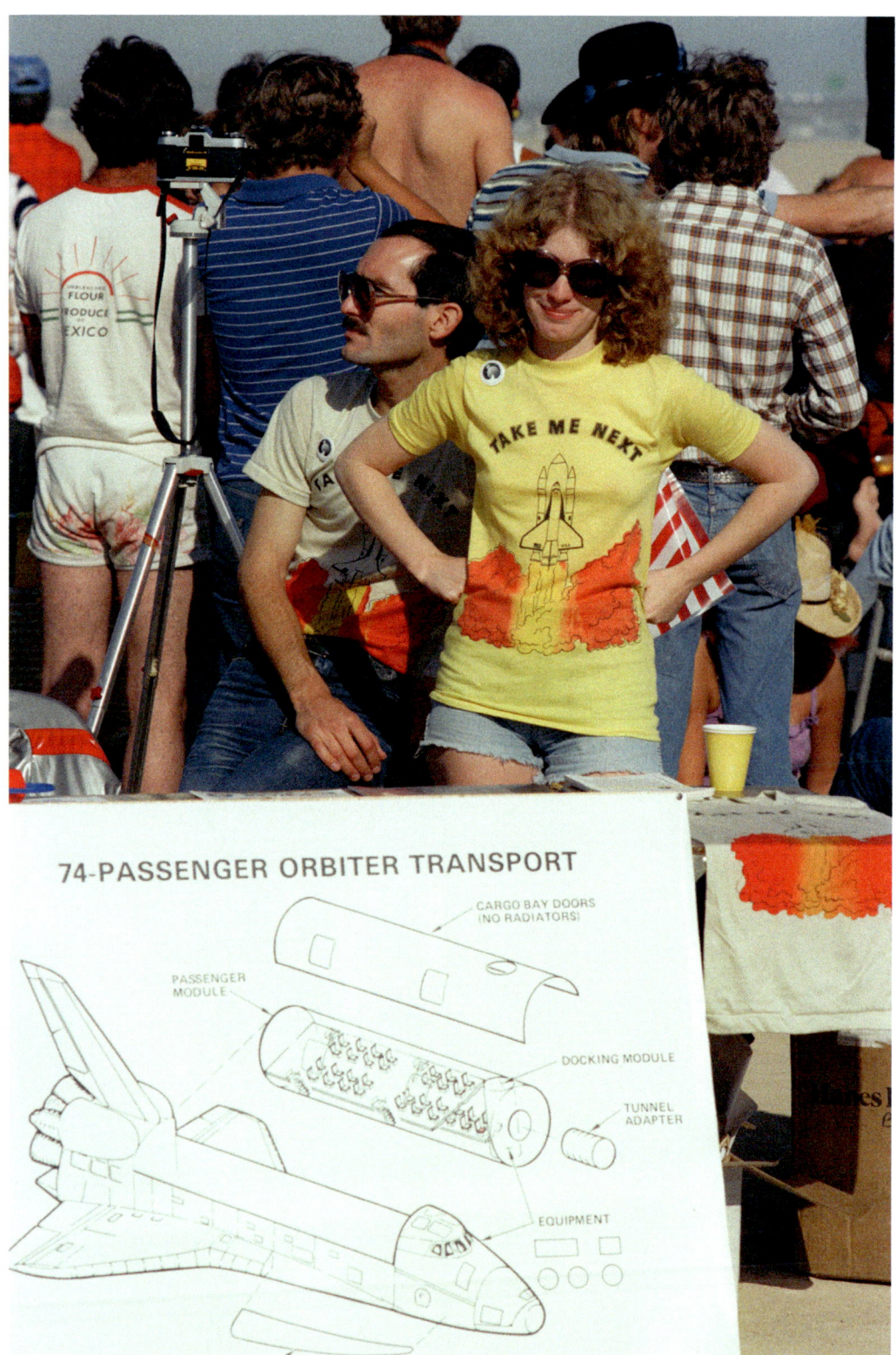

Take Me

Mission Accomplished

Final Orbit

Ready

In Position

Tuned In

89

Fly Navy

Good Grief

Starstruck

Happy to Be Here

Perimeter Patrol

Murray's Maintenance

93

Worth the View

The Spaceship

On Final

Gear Down

Done

CPSIA information can be obtained
at www.ICGtesting.com
Printed in the USA
LVHW020155231120
672433LV00001B/16

9 781735 962702

"HOPE IS HERE!"
Romans 15:13 NIV

May the God of hope fill you with all joy and peace as you trust in him, so that you may overflow with hope by the power of the Holy Spirit.

Then they stopped at the stable. The animals were in their stalls. The manger that had been in the corner was now placed in the middle of the floor. Straw was stuffed into it. It made for the most beautiful crib Pablito had ever seen. The man and woman that he had seen on the road were lying on a bed of straw. The woman was obviously in pain. Then he saw the Father smile as He said, "My Son." A baby's cry was heard, and the smallest angel of heaven whispered the words that were felt throughout the world:

Pablito went with all speed back to heaven. He made his report to the BIG, BIG Man. That's when it happened. As if on cue, everything in heaven began to move. Angels began flying everywhere. Pablito saw the choir getting their instruments and taking off towards the earth. The praises that were heard at that moment became so thunderous that Pablito couldn't help but join in. "Praise to God in the highest and on earth let His will be done!" The Father turned to Pablito and said, "You're with me, little one!" Pablito found himself soaring to earth right next to the Father on one side, and on the other side was the Holy Spirit. There were other angels there too. Michael was there, and the hosts of heaven were right behind them. On the way down, they passed the brightest star Pablito had ever seen. "That's the signal!" he said. They stopped and heard the choir sing to a group of shepherds. Pablito had guessed right. The expressions on their faces were priceless.

As he was leaving the town, he passed a couple on the road into town. The young man was walking next to a donkey. The young woman was sitting astride the beast. It was obvious she was with child. They seemed very tired – as if they had been walking for miles. Pablito looked at the couple and knew that Hope was very near.

He flew through the adjoining buildings and stopped at the synagogue. There was a man praying there by the name of Simeon. Pablito heard him pray for salvation, for peace, for hope. Pablito whispered into his ear, "Hope is on the way!"

He then flew to the town and went to a stable. He looked around, taking note of the creatures that were there. His eyes stopped on a manger in the corner. That manger would hold the baby Jesus. To the animals, he whispered, "Hope is on the way."

He went to a field. There, some shepherds were tending to their flock. *This is the place*, he thought. The choir will appear here! Everything is OK. He tried to imagine the surprise these shepherds were going to experience. This brought a smile to his face. He then whispered to them, "*Hope is on the way.*"

He flew to a place in the far east. There were some men looking through a telescope, looking for stars. Pablito whispered in their ears, "Hope is on the way."

Pablito flew down to earth with a speed he had never experienced before. He knew where he had to go. Everything needed to be perfect for the arrival of Jesus on earth. He didn't like the idea that Jesus was to be born in a stable. Jesus should be born in the greatest kingdom on earth and in the best bed, he thought, but God knew what He was doing; who was he to question the Creator?

Pablito was surprised when he heard the story, but if God said it, then that's the way it was going to happen. Now more than ever, he wanted to be a part of this event. Pablito wanted to help, but he wasn't a choir member; he couldn't help with any of the other plans; there was nothing Pablito could do to help. Pablito began to cry. He felt the touch of the Father's hand on his shoulder as He said, "Pablito, I was just going to look for you when you bumped into me." "Look for me?" he asked. "Why?" The Father said, "I have a special job for you. Only you can do this for me. I need someone to go down to earth and make sure everything is ready for my Son's arrival. I've already explained to you my plans, the where and when you already know. Would you go down and check for me? I would do it myself, but I am very busy, and I need someone to help me with this." Pablito almost screamed! God wants MY help! The BIG, BIG, Man is asking me to help Him. He blurted out, "Sure, God, whatever you need me to go, I will do, wherever you need me to go, I will go. I'll leave right away," and almost ran over the Father on his way out. The Father looked at the trail the little angel left and just smiled as He went over to begin what was to be the greatest time of earth's existence.

Then he heard the greatest story ever told by the BIG Man himself. He heard of how Jesus had volunteered to show the world how much God loved the people of the earth. He heard of the plan that God had formulated to redeem the people of earth of their sins. He learned that today would be the day that Jesus, being God, would be born as a child in a manger, in a little town called Bethlehem.

Pablito couldn't believe it! The BIG MAN knew his name and was standing right here in front of him. So he mustered up all the strength he could, and with a trembling voice and talking so fast he could hardly be understood, he asked God the question. "Excuse me, sir, do you know where Jesus is? Oh, but of course you do, you know everything. What I meant was, can you help me find Him or just tell me where He is? I need to ask Him a question." The Father said, "Slow down, Pablito, I do know where He is, but you can't see Him at the moment. He is helping me with a very important project. Maybe I can answer your question." God is actually talking to me, thought Pablito. "What's going on?" he asked. "Everyone seems to be getting ready for a big event. Nobody will tell me what it is. I try to help, and they just tell me to go away. I was hoping Jesus would tell me."

Pablito decided to look in the main mansion. That's where Jesus, the Holy Spirit, and the "BIG, BIG, MAN" lived. You know, the BIG, BIG, Man. That's what Pablito called Him. Sometimes Jesus would invite Pablito to the mansion, but he had never really seen the BIG, BIG, Man up close. Today he went through the expansive halls, hoping he wouldn't get lost. He had never been here alone. Jesus always led him around. Pablito went around a sharp corner and suddenly ran into something, or rather, someone. His face became enveloped in a robe. It was warm, soft, and a sweet perfume emanated from them. Stepping back a pace, Pablito looked up to see the owner of that robe. As he gazed upward, his mouth fell open in awe. There standing before him was the BIG, BIG, MAN Himself, and Pablito had just run into Him! He was going to that other place down there for sure! Nobody ran into the BIG, BIG, Man and lived eternally to tell about it! Pablito began to apologize for his actions, but the Father stopped him and said,

"No worries, Pablito, it was an accident."

Today he would get the answers he sought. He knew someone that would never say no to him. He should have thought of Him before. He would get his answer from Jesus, Himself. So off he went in search of Jesus. He went to the usual places, like the Throne Room and the Seat of Glory, but he didn't find Him there. Then he looked in the garden with the big beautiful trees that gave fruits at all times, but He wasn't there. Next, he looked in the choir practice room. Jesus liked to listen to the choir when they were practicing, but the choir was getting ready today, just like they had been doing for a while. Pablito asked the choir director, "Do you know where Jesus is? I want to ask Him a question." The choir director just looked at him and said, "Please go away, today is the day of our greatest performance, and we need to practice one last time. I don't have time for such a silly question." He sent Pablito away. Where was Jesus? Why couldn't Pablito find Him? It wasn't like Jesus to be away for so long.

Special was the last thing he felt for the past few days. Every angel was so busy doing this and doing that. Even his angel buddies couldn't play with him because they were called upon to help for the big moment. What was the big moment? Pablito tried to find out. Try he did but to no avail. Everyone he approached would tell him they were too busy or that he was too small to help. He was too small, but he didn't expect to stay that way too long. Someday he would be somebody. Someday he would be a big angel. Maybe he would become a cherub and stand at the throne, or a seraph and fly back and forth, working for Jesus, or even an archangel, a warrior angel, like Michael!

Pablito was the smallest angel in heaven, and he loved every bit of it. Sometimes as he passed the mansions that lined the streets of heaven, he would hear some of the other angels point to him and say, "There goes the smallest angel in heaven." He felt happy when he heard them because that meant he was special.

Little Pablito awoke with a start! He rose from his sleeping area to get ready for the day. The night before, preparations for an event were taking place, but he had been too busy playing to find out what that would be. He remembered seeing the father of his buddy Tito getting ready for something big, but when Pablito approached to ask a question, he was quickly dismissed and told to go play. So that's what he did. Play all day, play all night, with some worship of God in between, of course. That's the way Pablito spent his time up here in heaven.

Hope Is On The Way
© 2020 by Luis Velázquez
Illustrated by Jason Velázquez

All rights reserved solely by the author. The author guarantees all contents are original and do not infringe upon the legal rights of any other person or work. No part of this book may be reproduced in any form without the permission of the author. The views expressed in this book are not necessarily those of the publisher.

Printed in the United States of America.
ISBN-13: 978-1-7359627-0-2

All Scripture quotations, unless otherwise indicated, are taken from the Holy Bible, New International Version®, NIV®. Copyright ©1973, 1978, 1984, 2011 by Biblica, Inc.™ Used by permission of Zondervan. All rights reserved worldwide. www.zondervan.com The "NIV" and "New International Version" are trademarks registered in the United States Patent and Trademark Office by Biblica, Inc.™

Three Arrows
PUBLISHING

Long Island, New York

HOPE IS ON THE WAY

By Luis Velázquez

Illustrated by Jason Velázquez

*To Amalia,
Many Blessings*

1 Ptr 2:9